ALL ARE WELCOME

For all the teachers, librarians, and students who
make their schools a welcoming place to learn and grow
— AP & SK

THIS BOOK is inspired by Suzanne's daughters' school, Kimball Elementary, Seattle, USA, where diversity and community are not just protected, but celebrated. Suzanne created a poster for Kimball teachers to welcome all to their school, and the poster spread to other schools and communities throughout the United States. When Alexandra saw the image, it reminded her of the schools in her community in Brooklyn. She couldn't get the characters out of her mind and one late night sat down to write this story. We hope *All Are Welcome* is a celebration of diversity, and gives encouragement and support to all children.

BLOOMSBURY CHILDREN'S BOOKS
Bloomsbury Publishing Plc
50 Bedford Square, London, WC1B 3DP

BLOOMSBURY, BLOOMSBURY CHILDREN'S BOOKS and the Diana logo are trademarks of Bloomsbury Publishing Plc

First published in the USA in 2018 by Knopf Doubleday Publishing Group, 1745 Broadway, New York, NY 10019

This edition published in 2019 by Bloomsbury Children's Books, 50 Bedford Square, London WC1B 3DP

Text copyright © Alexandra Penfold 2018
Illustrations copyright © Suzanne Kaufman 2018

Alexandra Penfold and Suzanne Kaufman have asserted their rights under the Copyright, Designs and Patents Act, 1988,
to be identified as the Author and Illustrator of this work

A CIP catalogue record for this book is available from the British Library

ISBN: HB: 978-1-5266-0408-8; PB: 978-1-5266-0407-1; eBook: 978-1-5266-0406-4

8 10 9

Printed in Great Britain by Bell & Bain Ltd, Glasgow

All papers used by Bloomsbury Publishing Plc are natural, recyclable products from
wood grown in well managed forests. The manufacturing processes conform to
the environmental regulations of the country of origin

To find out more about our authors and books visit www.bloomsbury.com and sign up for our newsletters

Alexandra Penfold   Suzanne Kaufman

ALL ARE WELCOME

BLOOMSBURY
CHILDREN'S BOOKS
LONDON OXFORD NEW YORK NEW DELHI SYDNEY

Pencils sharpened in their case.
Bells are ringing, let's make haste.
School's beginning, dreams to chase.

All are welcome here.

No matter how you start your day.
What you wear when you play.

Or if you come from far away.

All are welcome here.

In our classroom safe and sound.
Fears are lost and hope is found.

Raise your hand, we'll go around.

All are welcome here.

Gather now, let's all take part.
We'll play music, we'll make art.

We'll share stories from the heart.

All are welcome here.

Time for lunch – what a spread!
A dozen different kinds of bread.
Pass it round till we're all fed.

All are welcome here.

Open doors, rush outside.
We will swing, we will slide.
We'll have fun side by side.

All are welcome here.

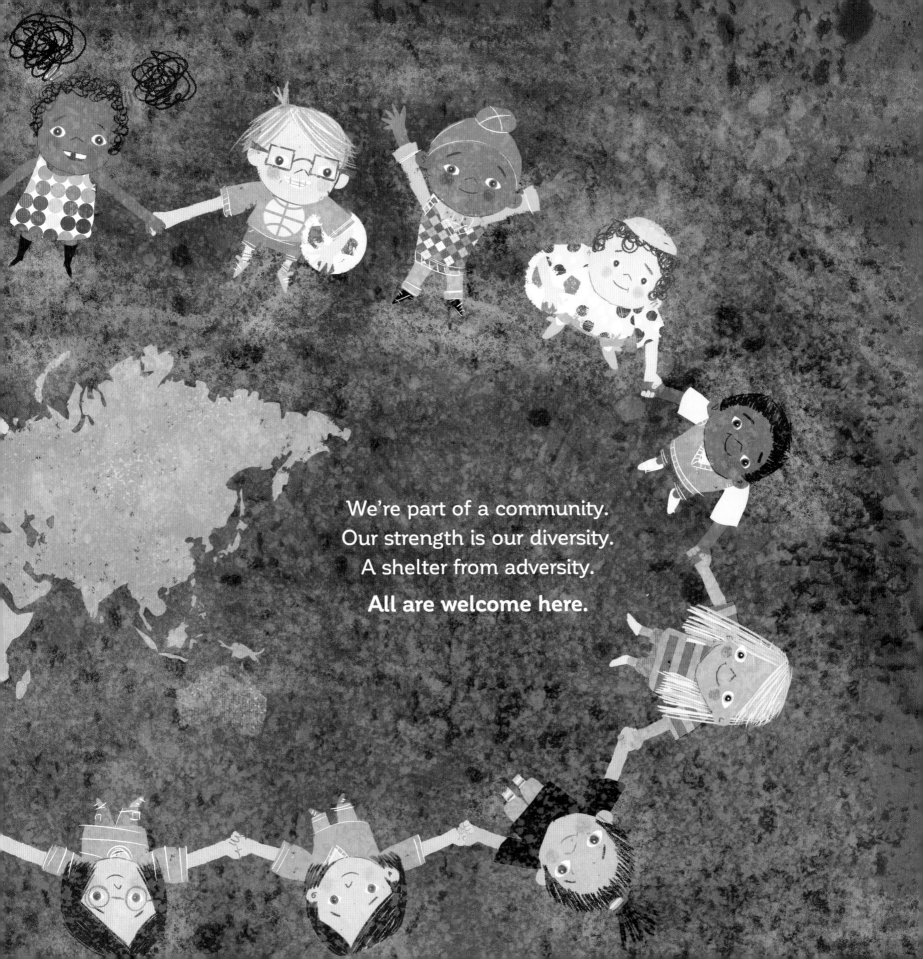

We're part of a community.
Our strength is our diversity.
A shelter from adversity.

All are welcome here.

We will learn from each other.
Special talents we'll uncover.

There's a big world to discover.

All are welcome here.

So much to learn, so much to do.
And when the busy day is through,

Can't wait to come back, start anew.

All are welcome here.

Head for home to get some rest

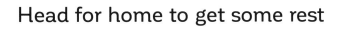

and greet tomorrow, ready and fresh.

Our time together is the best.

All are welcome here.

You have a place here.

You have a space here.

You are welcome here.